Magically Acquainted

Other Titles by Claire Burbank

WWW.CLAIREBURBANK.COM

Bullying(The Bully Book)

Claire Burbank Book Collection V1

Claire Burbank Book Collection V2

Five Crows

Sassy Tomatoes

Mo Lemont

Loop of Dreams

Magically Acquainted

I'm Not Invited

Magically Acquainted

Claire Burbank

BURBANK VENTURES LLC
NOTTINGHAM, NH

1.

Sky

Sixth grade was a crazy year. A lot of things happened, and I learned a lot. Hi, I'm Sky. I'm a unicorn. My best friend is a mermaid named Nora. There's just one thing. I'm really shy and she's really OUTGOING. And I mean REALLY shy and REALLY outgoing. If we were to go to a place with brand new people (which we basically did in middle school), I wouldn't want to go and Nora would. Which is the exact situation that happened in fifth grade. Fifth grade might have a lot of changes, but so does sixth grade.

You might be wondering how

unicorns and mermaids go to the same school. There is a whole system that we have. If you are a unicorn, a pegasus, or a fairy, you can just go to school. If you're a mermaid or seahorse, you learn on the right side of the hallway. The hallway is split up into two sections. The on-land section, and the in-water section. (*Clever names*, I know.) You can still communicate between sections, but you can't be in the same class as a mermaid if you're part of the on-land section. The on-land section is taught by dragons and griffons, while the in-water section is taught by seahorses.

Now you might think that this school is harmless, a magical peaceful place, but you're wrong. You're officially "uncool" if you are friends with someone who is from a different section. The problem is that Nora doesn't care about that stuff…but I do. I just want to be a normal unicorn. One who isn't noticed by anyone, and not teased about being friends with a mermaid.

2.

Nora

Sky needs to *relax*! She shouldn’t care about stuff like that! Our fellow students shouldn’t be judging us by our friends! Oh! By the way, I’m Nora the mermaid. And I LOVE meeting new people! When I met Sky, she was kind of scared of me. I thought there was something wrong, so I said, “Are you okay?” She just backed away.

When I asked her what she liked to do, she didn’t reply. I told her I liked playing in the water (we were at the beach for a preschool meet-and-greet). She finally looked at me and quietly said: “Me too.”

So, we played in the water together, starting our friendship. My favorite subject in fifth grade was learning about humans. They actually walk on two legs while unicorns walk on four legs, fairies fly, and mermaids and seahorses swim. Fifth grade was interesting and different, but sixth grade was even more interesting and different. There was more bullying, less kindness.

I remember the first day of fifth grade perfectly. Sky and I both felt so smart moving on to middle school and leaving the people in the grade below us. We had lockers for the first time, we got to switch classes, and we got to make new friends! But now that everyone knows each other…it's not that easy.

3.

Sky

Fifth grade was fun. We had barely any homework, everyone either made friends with you or didn't talk to you (I prefer the second one), and I was pushed around less.

Nora has always been the outgoing one that always stood up for me. Until Felicia the fairy came along.

Our school was calm. Our school was peaceful. Our school was kind. Until the new kid came to school. Her name was Felicia Dankie.

She might have been small, but boy, was she vicious! I just wanted to flick her across the room, but I knew that if

I did I would get in trouble. Plus, even if I were allowed to, I wouldn't have the courage, strength, or fingers for it. I will gladly tell you the story of how I met Felicia. I mean, if you want to, you don't have to listen if you don't want to…

It was the first day of school. There was a whole jumble of sixth graders scattered across the hallways of the school. I didn't recognize many creatures in the land section, and by the looks of it, I only recognized few mermaids and mermen in the water section (including Nora). This was probably because a lot of new kids joined the school.

Lots of my friends either waved to me (with their hoof or hand) or nodded their horn at me. Like Blossom the fairy, Mythica the unicorn, and Barb the Pegasus. In Barb's case, she greeted me by flapping her wing and nodding her head at me.

I suddenly got a jealous glare from an angry looking fairy. I opened my mouth to say something, but I was too shy and startled for anything to escape from my vocal cords. I mean, what would I say? Welcome to the school? Why are you glaring at me?

I looked on the other side of the hallway to see if Nora was watching, but she had already entered her classroom.

That reminded me that I had to get to class. I grabbed my stuff and headed off to science.

4.

Nora

When I headed to human studies I looked over to Sky to see if she was looking back. When she didn't, I just started swimming to my class.

"I wonder what sixth grade will be like," I thought. "Maybe—"

Suddenly a rude seahorse bumped into me. She had blue eyes, was pink, and was holding a seaphone up to her ear.

When I apologized, she just scoffed at me and said, "*Great* first impression, mermaid."

I widened my eyes and blinked back my tears. Today was going to be a good day, bumped into or not.

I took the seaweed seat closest to the middle, so I would hear the teacher but not get called on. I *am* the outgoing one between Sky and me, but participating in class is *not* my style.

"Hello, class!" the teacher

announced to the students. He was an orange seahorse with glasses and a big smile. “I’m Mr. Nerdicus your new teacher!”

“Eh-hem!” I heard someone clear their throat as Mr. Nerdicus wrote his name on the board with a rock. “EH-HEMM!”

I looked behind me and there she was. The seahorse that bumped into me in the hallway.

She chewed gum loudly as she whispered, “Can you, like, duck down, cuz’ your big head is blocking my view MERMAID.”

“We can switch seats,” I replied.

“No!” she answered. “What part of *duck down* do you NOT understand? You had a smaller brain than I thought.”

“Be nice, be nice, be nice,” I thought as I came up with something to say.”

"No thank you, SEAHORSE," I said to her.

She didn't talk to me for the rest of the day.

5.

Sky

As I tried to pick the right seating choice, I analyzed the room. Who should I sit next to? Will it be the right choice? Will the seating be permanent?

I was about to sit next to Mythica, when *ZOOM!* Felicia took my seat. I was sad. I was embarrassed. I was **ANGRY**. I ended up sitting next to two annoying griffons named Beau and Joe. I was hoping they weren't permanent when…

"Hello class, my name is Ms. Fireshooter and I'm your new educator!" a dragon standing at the front of the room exclaimed. "These will be your seats for the rest of the year, so hopefully you chose wisely."

Felicia turned her head around just to smirk at me with pride.

What was her problem?! I didn't do anything wrong! What was the matter with her? Had she previously been bullied? Whatever it was, I didn't want to know. I also didn't want to know if she would keep bullying me.

6.

Nora

As I went on with the rest of my day, one time the rude seahorse got called on by a teacher. I found out her name is Rhimestone. Too bad a pretty name was owned by a not-so-pretty-souled seahorse.

Later that day I saw Sky in the hallway. I waved to her, but she didn't wave back. Was it because of that *uncool* thing again? Or was she bullied, too? I bet it was both.

I know, you're probably like, "Woah, how did she know that?" if you're a human that's reading this. Or, if you studied mermaids before, you're like, "Yep. They can do that."

"What? What is it? They can do **WHAT**?" I can hear the first group of people who don't know mermaidology shouting.

"Just listen to her!" the second group that studied mermaids is replying.

The explanation is…that mermaids are psychic. We can tell what someone is thinking by looking at their face. Just another amazing thing we mermaids can do.

Remember when I said that Rhimestone didn't talk to me for the rest of the day? She might have not talked to me for the rest of the day, but the faces she made at me were fierce!

When we were in swimming class (unicorns, pegasi, and fairies have gym), Rhimestone and I were racing to see who was the fastest (teacher's choice). When I won, she gave me the nastiest look I ever saw. If her look were to speak, it would say: *You may be fast, but your brain is stupid, MERMAID!* She demanded to race again (she was talking to the gym teacher, not to me), and I won once again!

When she gave me another look that showed some things I shouldn't share, I decided not to race her again. After swimming lessons, we always swim into the lake, our home, and there is a pool pick up system. The PPUS is a system where parents swim to a specific spot and escort their kid to their seashell, or as humans, unicorns, and fairies call it, a house. For the on-land section, they have a bus that has four wheels that takes you to your house, or for fairies, your tree. Also, pegasi just fly to their homes in a group. I learned in Human Studies that humans also use buses. I think the in-water transportation system is easier and more convenient, but that's probably because I've never used the human/unicorn/fairy's system.

7.

Sky

After class, I saw Nora wave at me. I was about to wave back to trick her into thinking there wasn't anything wrong, but I suddenly remembered that mermaids are psychic. So, I didn't wave back, for there was no point in hiding my emotions.

Even if Felicia hadn't bullied me, I wouldn't have waved. Why? Because it's uncool to be friends with someone on the opposite side of the hallway, remember? I know she probably already told you about her whole psychic thing and how I was bullied and trying to be unnoticeable. The next on-land class was lunch. I usually sat with Blossom, Mythica, and Barb, but there were only ten people allowed at a table…and there were nine people already sitting there. I was about to sit with my friends, when guess who stole my seat again? FELICIA!

I thought Nora was *so* lucky. That she had no trouble with bullying or seating arrangements. I had to sit with a teacher sitting with me out of pity. She ate loudly and burnt my lunch when she sneezed. She was a dragon. I had no idea what Nora was also going through.

The absolute WORST part of that day, though…was the homework. My teachers gave me homework on the first day of school!

“I bet mermaids and seahorses don’t have homework,” I thought.

If I was ever feeling down, I would

go to the beach to see Nora about my problems. The problem was that I was SUPER ticked off, so my personality was opposite of what it usually was. Loud, bold, and rude.

"Nora!" I whined, galloping on the sand to the water.

When I arrived, breathless, my bestie replied, "What is it, Sky?"

"I had the worst day today!" I shouted in a raged manner. "This FAIRY, apparently named Felicia, was rude to me, took my seat twice, and was a complete meanie! I also have bundles of homework!"

"Oh, well my day was—" Nora started to say.

"—and for lunch I had to sit with a teacher that ate loudly and burnt my food when she sneezed! Felicia got my friends to laugh at me about it and I was really embarrassed! They could hear the teacher talking about dragon science to me, it was awful!" I complained speedily and run-on-sentence-ish.

"Well what happened with my day was—"

"You're so lucky that you get to be a part of your side of the hallway, you don't need to brag about it to me so just listen to me!" I shouted so loudly that it echoed everywhere.

I was not a friend. I didn't listen to her like she was listening to me. She tried to tell me how she was struggling like me, but I didn't let her. I was a terrible person. It definitely was not one of my nicest moments.

Nora said nothing and swam away after my latest outburst.

At the moment, I didn't understand why she was upset…so I got upset.

"Why did she just leave?!" I shouted to myself angrily.

I galloped to my house to tell my parents all about it. I thought I was the good guy in this situation. My mom is a unicorn and my dad is a Pegasus. They helped me understand the mess I made.

"IT'S NOT FAIR!" I screamed as I entered my house. "NO ONE UNDERSTANDS ME, NOT EVEN NORA!"

"Calm down Sky!" Mom told me. "What happened?"

Dad started coming downstairs as I started explaining.

I explained my whole day accurately up until the Nora incident.

"—and then I went to talk to Nora about my day. I explained it all to her just like I did to you, but then she just swam away!" I finished.

What I meant by not *accurately* was that I just didn't give off much detail.

"But WHY did she swim away?" Mom asked.

"I…don't know," I lied.

"We all know you're not a very good actress, sweetie," Dad teased.

"Fine," I replied. "I *might* have come off a little bit too strong."

"Yeah," Mom answered. "We could hear you shouting from here."

My face suddenly turned red.

"Maybe she swam away because her feelings were hurt," my dad correctly assumed. "Did you say something that if she said it to you, you would feel sad?"

"I might have kind of said that she shouldn't brag about her awesome day and just let me talk…" I sheepishly retorted.

"What if her day wasn't so peachy either?" Mom asked.

"Then I would feel terrible," I said. "Even if she didn't have a good day, I should apologize tomorrow."

8.

Nora

I was upset. This wasn't the Sky that I knew. She thought I didn't understand and that my day was better. I felt like I was forbidden to speak. Like I was in a nightmare where I had no voice. I didn't feel like I was in a *friend* position. I decided to ignore everyone at school the next day the bully, my so-called *friend*, my classmates. Just like Sky ignored my day at school. I didn't think she would want to talk to me anyway. I had thought she was in her own selfish little world. I didn't even want to read her mind that day.

I swam through the hallway, blank-faced. It was *Terrible Tuesday*, I thought.

You might think I was being dramatic, and that I was being selfish. The truth is, we had never fought like that before. I was usually the outgoing one. To be in the position where I couldn't speak…it was awful. I didn't want to be the shy one. I wanted to stand up for myself. I don't think I could handle a bully *and* a friend who put me in that position. I couldn't trust anyone, but I *could* ignore everyone.

I was focused on two things: not talking to anyone and getting to class.

I heard my name being shouted from across the hallway by a familiar voice. I kept staring forward, ignoring Sky's shouts.

"Get your human studies shellbook

and get to class," I repeated inside my head.

"Hey, Nora!" some mermaids and seahorses exclaimed.

I was almost there when Rhimestone stopped me in my tracks. "Not so fast, NORA."

I tried to get past her, but she wouldn't let me get to class. I tried being kind.

"Excuse me, can I please get to class? I had a rough day yesterday, and—" I started to say.

"—oh, WAH, WAH!" Rhimestone interrupted in a superior voice. "You had a rough day! Oh no, did you tell King Triton about your worries and woes? You POOR THING."

"Just let me get to class!" I shouted, starting to get angry.

"Oh, you wouldn't want to be tardy

with your perfect attendance and all that?" she replied.

I couldn't stop the few tears that ran down my cheeks.

"Just please let me get through," I whispered quietly, head down, so no one could hear the melancholy in my voice.

First the rudeness, then the bad sportsmanship, now this?

"Fine, but only because you're a baby and I wouldn't want to get in trouble for making you go '*WAH, WAH*'!" she answered, followed by a laugh that you would expect to come out of a pink seahorse.

I felt betrayed, weak, and lonely. Apparently, I was uncool (said by Sky), a baby (said by Rhimestone), and not myself (said by me).

Sky was my #1 friend. No one else really understood my full-time ecstasy and outgoing-ness. I was really upset. What could make it better? Nothing at the time.

Until I actually got to class. Let me explain.

The day before, Monday, was the day that the teacher tested our skills on humans. Mr. Nerdicus wanted us to draw pictures of humans, and whoever did the best got a prize. I found out that I won the prize! It was a…toy fish made out of seaweed? I bet he literally took a chair, took some strands of seaweed off it, and sculpted it into this *toy fish*.

"Wow…" I said, unimpressed. "Thank you…I'm honored!"

By the way, I wasn't honored. I was still in the same mood I was in before. Upset.

9.

Sky

That was a sad Tuesday. And not only because it was the second day of school. Ugh! Nora had ignored me the whole day, and I also had bullying problems of my own.

I was clueless. I had no idea how upset, hurt, and weak my best friend was.

As I was trying to get Nora's attention so I could apologize, Felicia was passing by.

"You have a little underwater friend, huh?" she teased after taking a picture of me trying to get Nora's attention. "Hah, I'm sending this to the whole school!"

My face suddenly turned blank and pale like I was going to puke. But I wasn't. I was silently crying and screaming inside. I just wanted to be unnoticed by everyone but Nora, but it turned out to be the opposite situation. My life was turned around—and on the second day of school.

I suddenly felt a vibration from my phone in my backpack (I'm assuming you humans know what that is). I immediately knew what it was, but I hoped that it wasn't what I thought it was. I took out my phone and instantly wondered how she sent it to every student in the on-land section so quickly. I opened my text message app and dreaded what I saw. It wasn't only the picture, it was the caption that went along with it.

She texted: "Sky with her little

mermaid friend! *TOTALLY not uncool*! LOL! Btw, that was sarcastic!"

I could just hear her sarcastic, cocky voice ringing in my head. Especially the word *uncool*.

"You know what?" I said to myself. "Who cares if I'm uncool? I just have to get my friend back!"

I was determined. Nora would be my friend again by the end of the day. I just had to get her attention. I figured the only time of day to do it was after school. I went to the ocean to see…no one.

"Of course," I thought. "Why would she come here when she wouldn't talk to me at school?"

I grabbed my phone and dialed Nora's home phone. I had a plan.

"Hello?" Nora's mom answered as she picked up the seaphone.

“Hi, it’s Sky,” I greeted. “Is Nora there?”

“Um, hold on a second,” she retorted.

I heard some whispering from the other end of the phone.

“She’s uh, in the—” my best friend’s mother started to say, “the bathroom.”

“Pardon me, but I know she’s not in the bathroom,” I told her. “I just want to talk to her.”

“Well, you caught me,” she said. “I’ll try to convince her, but don’t count on it, sweetie. I don’t want you to be out there for a while.”

“I won’t,” I promised.

About seven minutes later, I heard some splashing in the water. It was Nora!

“Nora!” I exclaimed.

Her face was wearing a melancholy-like expression.

"I'm *really* sorry," I apologized. "I was struggling with a bully, unkindness, and—enough about me, though. Tell me about your problems."

Nora explained to me all of her problems, and then I told her mine.

"I'm sorry," we both said a bajillion times.

Nora felt bad about ignoring me in school, and I felt bad about the whole situation. We were friends again, and that's all that mattered.

10.

Nora

Although we mermaids can read minds, I had no idea what Sky was also going through. We had both apologized, and we could go to each other for our problems since we were in similar situations.

It wasn't Woeful Wednesday, it was Wonderful Wednesday. I was feeling more outgoing, and I had a plan. Sky and I were both taking magic (or spell-making as the on-landers called it), but the teacher that I had taught me a specific spell that I thought would help us with our problems. It was an "anti-bullying" spell. It protected you from any insults or bad comments coming your way by wearing a special necklace. It contained these ingredients: light from angler fish, sea urchins, anemone, pearls, and sand from the deepest, darkest, cave in the sea. These ingredients were very hard to find, but my dad and I ended up finding everything and conjuring the spell together. When he asked what the spell was for, I told him it was for homework.

I put them in the necklaces and gave one to Sky before school that day. We made the spell on Tuesday after I did my real homework.

I went to school with a confident smile on my face, swimming proudly across the hallway. I saw Rhimestone approach me as I glided across the hallway.

"Hey merm—" she started to say. "Merm—merm!"

The spell was working!

"Bye, Rhimestone!" I teased, swimming away.

"Wait you dum—duh—" the seahorse tried to add.

"What is this sorcery?"

I silently cheered inside. I was bully free! I looked over to the on-land section and saw Sky confidently walking and a fairy trying to bully her but struggling in attempting to do it. It was working for her, too! Success!

11.

Sky

Nora's spell worked perfectly! I felt more confident than I ever had in my life. I wasn't that shy, little unicorn anymore! I was proud of being unique.

Since Felicia sent out my message, everyone wanted to pick on me.

"Hey Sky, I saw the picture of you and your little mermaid friend!" a pegasus said as he approached me. "Lam—lay—what's happening?!"

I smiled as I walked away from the choking horse with wings. He couldn't tease me! SO COOL!

"Your reputation is almost as

crooked as your hor—" a fairy started to say. "Your hor—"

I knew she was trying to say horn, but I just enjoyed the silence.

Only two other creatures tried to tease me and failed. All of the others didn't want to be seen with me except for Blossom, Mythica, and Barb. Life was going swell. Well, at least until music class.

"Welcome to my classroom, young musicians!" Mrs. Ruth exclaimed as my classmates and I entered the room. "Today, we are going to be playing the recorders."

My necklace suddenly started getting itchy. My spell-making teacher *did* say that when jewelry magic starts running out, it begins to get itchy. I didn't know what to do, so I just took it off and asked the teacher if I could go put it in my backpack which was in the hallway. She agreed, so I went to carefully place my valuable anti-bullying necklace in my bag which held the most homework I had ever had on the third day of school. I was studying the itchy string when I tripped on a backpack. The piece of jewelry immediately slipped out of my hooves as I saved myself from falling on my face. The jewel that held the magic shattered into seven little pieces as the magic that was left from it fogged up a little amount of air.

"No!" I cried, but not loud enough for my classmates to hear. "The necklace!"

I picked up the remains and galloped to the nearest trash can located at the end of the hallway. I threw them in the trash and went back to the classroom. By the time I got back, everyone had already gotten their recorders.

“Where were you?” the teacher asked suspiciously. “Fooling around?”

“No miss,” I answered. “Um…zipper troubles…you know, with my backpack.”

She nodded and pointed to the recorders. I gloomily retrieved one as everyone else played “music”. I was too distracted with what just happened to hear the ear-shrieking noises coming out of those instruments.

“I just broke the magic my best friend worked so hard to make! Also, I’m going to be torn apart by my fellow classmates!” I thought. “I have to tell Nora! Remember the friend code: *No guys, no lies, no denies, or goodbyes*.”

No one teased me for the rest of the day because they were scared, but they would forget about it by the next day. Sixth grade wasn't easy, and it wasn't getting easier.

12.

Nora

The necklace was working perfectly the whole day, except for when it started to get itchy, which was perfectly normal. Everything was great, before was just a *beginning of school drama fest*.

I wasn't expecting a panicked Sky to approach me at the beach.

"What is it?" I asked, hoping the cycle wasn't starting over again.

"I might have made a mistake," Sky answered sheepishly.

"What happened?" I questioned.

"Uh, I sort of kind of accidentally…" she started to say. Her voice suddenly became really quiet. “Broke the magic necklace…”

“What did you say?” I asked. “That was kind of quiet.”

“I broke your magic necklace!” Sky admitted so fast that it was like ripping off a bandage.

“REALLY?!” I shouted, teasing her. “Are you kidding me, that’s totally…fine.”

“Really?” she sighed, relieved and surprised.

“I mean, we were just testing it out,” I assured her. “And I know it was an accident.”

Her face changed from stunned to happy.

“You know what?” Sky suggested. “We just need to relax.”

“I agree,” I replied. “It hasn’t even

been a week yet, and we've gone through the stress of a whole year!"

"Yeah, we're only *half way through* the first week," she added.

"It's going to be a crazy year," I predicted. "That's for sure."

13.

Sky

That Thursday wasn't any less crazy and hectic than the first three days of sixth grade. It proved that I was the odd one out, and that I wasn't popular.

It all started when school began at 8:00. I saw everyone in the on-land section looking at their phones and smiling with faces of excitement. I looked at the in-water section and saw everyone also looking at their seaphones.

"What's going on?" I asked Blossom. "I don't understand."

"You didn't get the message?" my fairy friend asked. "Felicia is throwing a back-to-school party on Friday, and it looks like she's inviting the whole school!"

"Well, not me," I replied, my voice cracking a bit.

"Oh, I bet your phone just isn't connected to WIFI or something," she suggested. "Anyway, I've got to get to class."

"I think I know why I didn't get an invitation," I thought as I walked away.

I was wondering if Nora got the invitation, so I texted her.

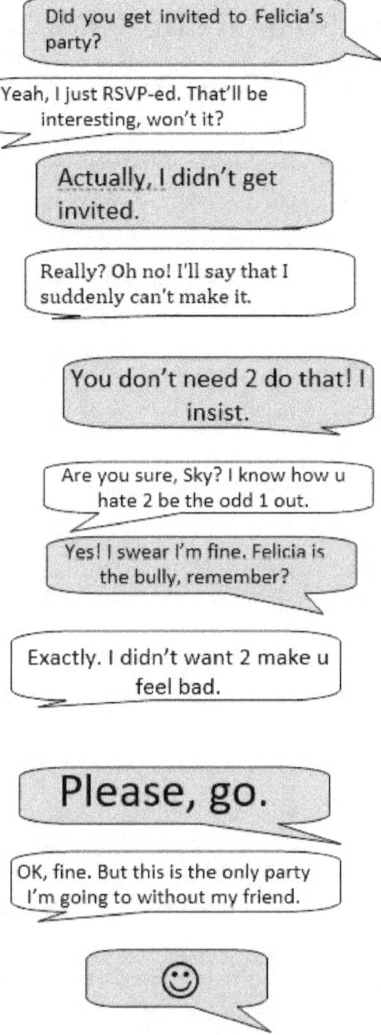

I couldn't keep Nora from going to the party after keeping her from speaking! I couldn't be a restrictive friend. If I was invited to a party with the whole school and Nora wasn't invited

I would still want to go. I had to put myself in her shoes.

14.

Nora

When I got the invitation from Felicia I was honestly excited. It was a back-to-school beach party with everyone there! When I found out Sky wasn't invited, I was upset. I didn't want to go that much anymore, but when she insisted, I gave in. I just didn't want to make her feel bad. The party was at 5:00 that Friday. This was the invitation:

After I texted Sky, I found out Felicia meant by the “whole” school. Sky was the only person in the WHOLE ENTIRE SCHOOL to not be invited. Felicia was a jerk. I finally decided not to go.

I'm not going to the Party

Why not? I thought u said u

Well, I was until I found out Felicia was a jerk.

Ya think?

Sorry I ever said I would

I feel bad 4 restricting u.

From now on, I'll let u make ur own decisions.

Thanks, Sky. That means a lot.

Friends again?

I felt good. We were friends again, for sure. I felt so good, that I did all of my homework for the weekend on that night. I guess I had a lot of energy! I had no idea what the next problem would be, but I knew we would always come back from it.

That weekend, Sky and I had another idea. We wanted to take action again, Plan B. We decided to use a spell. This spell, though, was Sky's idea. Her magic—or "spell making" teacher said it was called: "Moonlight Mix-up". She told me it was for switching bodies. I asked her why and what we were going to do with it, and she said we were going to expose the bullies by being in each other's shoes. Here's how she thought we could do it:

"So, we'll switch bodies with these special rings, which we can't take off while we're at school," she explained. "Since we have different personalities, we can approach Rhimestone and Felicia in different ways. I will become a mermaid and switch into your body, and you'll become a unicorn and switch into my body."

I thought it was a perfect plan and that we should start gathering the ingredients for Monday: blueberries, a daisy petal, a strand of golden string, a piece of wax from a cinnamon candle, and blue sea glass from Mystical Beach. Since I didn't know what half of those things were, I knew Sky would have to find them. So, I let her get all of the supplies while I made the ring molds. It took about two hours for us to finish. When we finally did on that sunny Saturday, we decided to test it out. Sky and I took the rings and we counted down from three.

"Three…two…one," we counted.

We slipped the rings on my finger and her hoof, and we felt a vibration. Our souls magically slipped out of our bodies and into each other's! It worked (obviously, we both had A+s in magic/spell making)!

It was the strangest feeling I ever experienced in my life! I was a unicorn! I had LEGS! And FOUR of them! I was like Ariel from The Little Mermaid!

It was like angelic, beautiful music was playing until it got suddenly cut off when I fell on the ground. I had never fallen on the ground before though, so I ended up on the ground, screaming and moving all four of my legs in a swimming motion. I looked really stupid. In fact, the most stupid I had ever looked in my life.

"This is so cool!" I exclaimed. "I'm actually on land!"

I looked over at Sky who was trying to swim but was failing. It was like I was looking at a less-inept-at-swimming mirror! I tried standing and balancing first, and then I attempted walking.

“Our plan is going to be great!” I shouted from the sand.

Sky was still underwater, so she stuck her arm out of the water with a big thumbs up. I wondered what her experience as an underwater creature was like.

15.

Sky

The moment I slipped the ring on my hoof it was like I was on a rollercoaster, my stomach turning and me screaming.

I was suddenly in the water with no trouble breathing at all. While I kept screaming, I couldn't hear gurgles, I didn't choke on the water, and I saw no water bubbles. It took be a couple of moments to realize I was a mermaid! I was breathing…UNDER WATER! It was a whole different feeling! This rollercoaster was virtual reality, 4 dimensional! But no…this was real life!

When I thought I was swimming perfectly and gracefully, I was really flopping around clumsily and faultily. My defectiveness was just as bad as Nora's, though. She was getting used to the land while I was getting used to the water.

"Okay, I want to be myself again," I demanded after failing a belly flop.

"Same," Nora agreed.

We counted down again followed by yanking off the rings. We both enjoyed our normal positions for the rest of the weekend.

Our plan started Monday morning, 7:15 A.M. We did it so early because I had to catch my bus. Nora had the "PPUS" so she was flexible. Instead of riding or transporting the way we usually did, we were going to switch places before school started.

We also needed the time for getting used to our new figures again and explaining to each other how our transportation systems worked.

It was weird being a mermaid again and going to the school with Nora's mom. She thought I was Nora, so it was difficult to have a conversation with her.

"Hey mom!" I exclaimed as I did what Nora said and caught up to her mother.

"Why did you have to meet Sky again?" she asked.

"Oh, to…" I started to say, trying to come up with something believable. "…do some homework!"

"I thought you had different classes and homework," Nora's mom replied. "You know, you study different things since you're two different types of creatures."

"First, don't call us creatures!" I answered, totally sounding like Nora.

"Second, it was a back to school assembly thing."

"Oh, okay," she understood.

"Yes!" I thought. "I convinced her! That was kind of easy."

I arrived at school amazed and proud of myself for accomplishing it. It was a brand-new approach at things.

"Let's see…Rhimestone," I thought. "Hmm…there she is! Okay, nice approach, nice approach."

"Out of my way, mermaid!" Rhimestone exclaimed when I *accidentally* got in her way.

"Oh, I'm sorry, I didn't see you there," I apologized in my shyest voice. "I'll try to stay out of your way next time."

"Huh?" she wondered out loud. "Why are you being so nice, I…no one has ever been nice to me before."

"Well, maybe we could be friends," I sympathized. "We could start over."

Hopefully Nora could take over where I left off.

"That would be nice," she agreed, tearing up a bit.

I had just made a new friend for someone! Got to check that one off the bucket list. I wondered how Nora was doing.

16.

Nora

When I got to school, I had finally gotten used to my four legs again. Being in the on-land section was strange. There were small fairies and big unicorns. How was I supposed to find a small fairy in a big place like that?

Right when I saw her blond hair, blue eyes, and sassy look on her face, I knew it was Felicia.

"Oh, talking to your little mermaid friend again, Sky?" she sassily commented.

She was messing with the wrong merm—unicorn.

"How 'bout you keep rolling those

eyes," I roasted her. "Maybe one day you'll find a brain back there."

Felicia blinked, eyes wide open and gaping. "You know what, I like your new style. Let's hang out."

"Maybe when you actually apologize," I replied, trying to be nicer and solve the problem.

"For what?" she asked in the most annoying valley-girl-ish voice I had ever heard.

"For bullying me," I stated the obvious after majorly cringing.

Suddenly she burst out in tears.

"I'm sorry!" she whisper-sobbed so no one would hear her sorrow. "I…I've been having a tough time with—with my family. I'm sorry I hurt your feelings, I've just been taking it all out on you."

"Felicia, as long as you don't do it anymore, I forgive you," I answered in the nicest voice I could. "And I'm sorry you've been having problems with your family."

She smiled. "Let's be friends."

I nodded in agreement.

She flew away to class. When everyone but Sky and I went to class, we texted each other about our accomplishments.

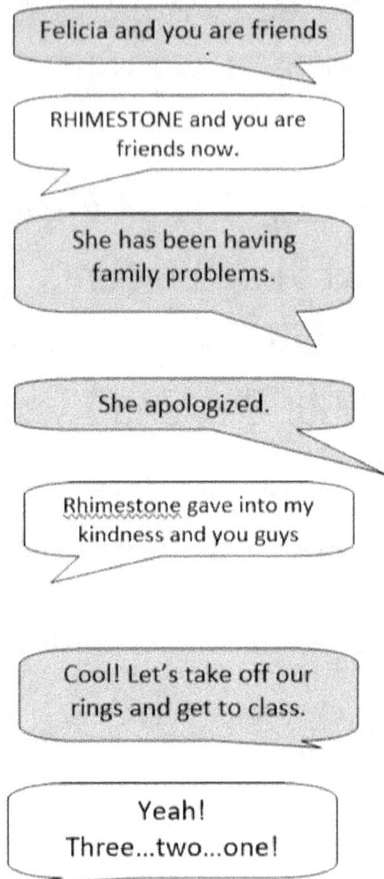

We looked at each other as we yanked the rings off our wrist and hoof.

I magically transported to the in-water section once again. It felt good to be a mermaid again. It also felt good to help someone let their feelings out and become their friend in my own way. I saw Rhimestone poke her head out of Mr. Nerdicus's door.

"You coming?" she asked me.

"Yep!" I exclaimed, starting to swim to class.

I smiled at Sky. We officially completed our mission.

"Now it's time to become closer as friends," I texted to Sky.

My best unicorn friend, BUF, texted back a thumbs up emoji. I laughed considering the fact we agreed, and the fact that she didn't even have thumbs. I quickly swam to my first class. Soon, my daily routine would include sitting with my new friend Rhimestone at lunch. Since Sky's personality was nice, I would try to be nice to Rhimestone.

"I think she'll let me be kind to her," I thought as I took a seat next to the pink seahorse that used to bully me. “If Sky can do it, I bet I can.”

17.

Sky

Being a unicorn again felt really good. I could get back to my four-legged schedule. One foot in front of the other. The only difference was that Felicia was my new friend. I had my arms wide open for a new friend. If she apologized, she was a worthy friend of mine.

I was surprised at how well our plan had worked. The beginning of the school year was a dramatic, lesson learning, adventurous experience, but I knew there was more adventure to come. I just had to be myself and be Magically Acquainted.

www.ingramcontent.com/pod-product-compliance
Lightning Source LLC
Chambersburg PA
CBHW070452170726
48291CB00005B/1718

* 9 7 8 1 9 4 9 7 0 1 0 3 6 *